The Bridge to Sharktooth Island

A Challenge Island
STEAM Adventure

D1173705

By Sharon Duke Estroff and Joel Ross

Illustrated by Mónica de Rivas

WEST
MARGIN
PRESS

Edited by Michelle McCann

Photo credits: Page 111: eilatan / Shutterstock.com; siwawut / Shutterstock.com; page 123 C2RMF: Galerie de tableaux en très haute definition

Library of Congress Cataloging-in-Publication Data

Names: Estroff, Sharon, author. | Ross, Joel N., 1968- author. | DeRivas, Mónica, illustrator.
Title: The bridge to Sharktooth island : a Challenge Island STEAM adventure/ by Sharon Duke Estroff and Joel Ross ; illustrated by Mónica de Rivas.
Description: [Berkeley, CA] : West Margin Press, [2021] | Summary: When Daniel, Joy, and Kimani suddenly find themselves stranded on a mysterious island, they must work together to find clues hidden around that somehow hold the key to finding their way back home. Includes STEAM related activities.
Identifiers: LCCN 2021009127 (print) | LCCN 2021009128 (ebook) |
    ISBN 9781513289533 (paperback) | ISBN 9781513289557 (ebook)
Subjects: CYAC: Islands--Fiction. | Cooperativeness--Fiction. | Resourcefulness--Fiction. | Problem solving--Fiction. | Cousins--Fiction.
Classification: LCC PZ7.1.E854 Br 2021 (print) | LCC PZ7.1.E854 (ebook) |
    DDC [Fic]--dc23
LC record available at https://lccn.loc.gov/2021009127
LC ebook record available at https://lccn.loc.gov/2021009128

Printed in China
25 24 23 22 21 1 2 3 4 5

Published by West Margin Press®

WEST
MARGIN
PRESS
WestMarginPress.com

Proudly distributed by Ingram Publisher Services

WEST MARGIN PRESS
Publishing Director: Jennifer Newens   Editor: Olivia Ngai
Marketing Manager: Angela Zbornik   Design & Production: Rachel Lopez Metzger
Project Specialist: Micaela Clark   Design Intern: Evie Jones

Dear Reader,

Welcome to Challenge Island, a magical place where engineering meets imagination! You are about to set sail on an exhilarating voyage to one of the many action-packed Challenge Islands. Each island comes with a unique set of problems that the Challenge Island kids have to solve—together! They have to be creative, using only what's in the treasure chest and their imaginations. After the story, at the back of the book, you will have a chance to try out the challenges with your own team at home!

Boom. Boom. Boom. Did you hear that? It sounds like the Challenge Island drums calling you. That means the adventure is about to begin. *Boom. Bada-boom!* There it is again. Sounds like it's time for us to get going full STEAM ahead!

Happy reading!
Sharon Duke Estroff
Co-Author and Founder/CEO of the Challenge Island
STEAM Program

Chapter 1

Sometimes magic happens in the most ordinary places.

There was nothing special about the city block or the basketball court. There was nothing special about the cars driving by on the street or the snowflakes falling from the sky.

The kids making the snowman didn't look special either—but they were.

"I'm freezing," the boy said, shoving his hands into his pockets.

"You're always freezing," the girl said.

"Only when you drag me outside in a snowstorm," the boy said.

His name was Daniel Perez. He was in fifth grade, and liked video games and sports, because he was *good* at video games and sports. He liked being good at things.

He was with his cousin, Joy. She was exactly ten days younger than he was, so everyone in the family called them 'the twins,' even though they looked nothing alike. Daniel was big for his age, with dark skin and straight hair. Joy was small, with reddish hair and sparkling blue eyes.

At school, Daniel sat quietly in class and played sports during recess. Joy fidgeted in class, and did flips on the jungle gym during recess. Joy loved taking risks. Sometimes Daniel thought she even loved messing up.

It was the first weekend in January, and snow covered the basketball court. Daniel had just hefted a medium-sized snowball onto a giant snowball, and his fingers were still numb.

"Now we just need to make her head," Joy told him.

She poked buttons into the snowman's middle. Well,

the snow*woman's* middle. Today, the snowperson was a girl. Joy had even snagged a flowery hat from her sister's closet for the finishing touch.

"We need a carrot," Daniel told her.

"I'd rather have a granola bar," Joy said.

"I mean for her nose."

"So do I." Joy unzipped her snow jacket halfway. "She's going to have a granola nose."

"You're weird," Daniel told her, not for the first time.

"I'm creative," Joy said. "I take after Grandma Day."

"Those are just stories," Daniel said. "We're not really the great-great-grandchildren of a wise woman with a talking scarf."

"I'm descended from the wise woman," Joy said. "*You're* descended from the scarf."

Daniel kicked snow at Joy, then watched her flap her coat to cool herself off. "How can you be hot?" he asked.

"Because I'm not just standing around."

"I'm not just standing around," he told her. "I'm also shivering."

"Making a snow-head will warm you up," she said, giving him a big-eyed, pleading look.

He snorted, then took his hands from his pockets and made a snowball. But he didn't roll it into a head. Instead, he eyed the basketball hoop. He faked left, spun right, then jumped and took a shot.

Swish! Nothing but net.

"Three points!" he yelled.

He took another shot, then started helping Joy make a head for the snowwoman. Goofing around outside was the best thing ever. Except winter break was almost over. School started again tomorrow.

"Last day of vacation," he moaned.

"Yeah," Joy said, shaping the snowwoman with a *scrape-pat-scrape.* "I guess we won't have time to make a whole snowperson parade."

Daniel stared at her. He hadn't known they were *trying* to build a snowperson parade.

After a second, he turned toward the street. The car noise was muffled by the snow but their tires rumbled

over a grate with a *clatter clank, clatter-clatter-clank*. Snowflakes landed on Daniel's cheeks. Starting tomorrow, he'd spend every day at the same desk, in the same room, doing the same worksheets. He'd have class then recess, then class, then lunch, then class, then recess, then class.

Nothing new ever happened. Nothing exciting.

He wished for something more. He wished for something different. And inside him, a tiny spark caught fire. Because sometimes, magic happens at the most ordinary times too.

After she packed the snow-head with a *pat-pat-pat,* Joy continued to shape the snowwoman with a *thup-thup-thup*, matching the rhythm of the street noise.

Then a louder rhythm began to fill the air:

Boom-badoom-doom-boom-ba-BOOM.

Boom!

Boom-badoom-doom-boom-ba-BOOM.

Boom!

Joy gasped. "What is that?"

"Sounds like..." Daniel blinked at the street. "...drums."

"A *thousand* drums," Joy said.

The music was fast and fierce and happy, and seemed to echo all around them. Daniel felt the rhythm pounding along with his heartbeat. The wintry morning suddenly smelled of sunshine and surf, like a hot summer's day at the beach.

Then the air shimmered and all the fluttering snowflakes turned bright blue, the color of a cloudless sky.

"D-do you see that?" Daniel whispered.

"Yeah." Joy grabbed his hand like when they were little, but for once he didn't mind.

Boom-badoom-doom-boom-ba-BOOM.

Boom-badoom-doom-boom-ba-BOOM.

The drums pounded louder and louder, faster and faster... until the drumbeat *whooshed* them into the air.

Daniel felt himself flying through the blue snowflakes, which tumbled around him like a kaleidoscope. He yelped in surprise and heard Joy shouting with glee.

The snow blurred and swirled until, in an instant,

it vanished.

The basketball court disappeared.

The block faded away.

The whole city was gone.

Daniel felt himself falling—down, down, down! But before he even had a chance to feel afraid, he landed as soft as a feather.

Though he wasn't in the snow anymore. He was on a small grassy hill, facing an endless sparkling ocean.

Everything else was gone—everything except Joy, who was standing beside him, her red hair blowing in the warm breeze.

Chapter 2

"**W**hoa." Joy gaped at the sun, hanging bright and golden above them. "The snowwoman doesn't stand a chance!"

"What?" Daniel stammered in shock. "What? What? What?"

"She'll melt!" Joy explained, stomping on the grass like she was checking if it was real. "It's summer here."

"Where?" he asked.

"Here!" Joy spun in a circle.

"But where's *here*?"

"Some ginormous boulder," she said, "smack dab in the

middle of the ocean."

When Daniel looked around, he saw that Joy was right. The small grassy hill was only one side of a craggy boulder the size of a basketball court. A stone outcropping jutted from the top like a chimney. The ocean sparkled in the sunlight ten feet below Daniel.

Waves shimmered and lapped at the bottom of the boulder and the air smelled salty. In the distance, Daniel spotted a chain of islands. Some rose high into the sky, and some spread low across the water. Some had jungles, some had mountains, and some were shrouded in mist. One looked like a huge volcano.

"Check this out," Joy called, climbing higher on the boulder.

"I *am* checking it out!" he said, looking at the chain of islands.

"Not that," she said. "Up here!"

When Daniel climbed up and joined her, he saw that the boulder they were on was just a stone's throw from an island with a white sand beach. Well, maybe *two* stones' throws. Leaves shimmered in the lush green forest that started behind the beach. Little birds darted across the sand, and the tide swirled around glistening rocks.

"We're not smack dab in the middle of the ocean," Daniel said, his voice hushed. "We're just off the shore of a tropical island!"

"My sister is going to be so jealous," Joy said gleefully.

"There are palm trees!" Daniel said, pointing at the beach. "With coconuts!"

"If those are coconuts," Joy told him, "then those trees must be coconut trees."

"There's no such thing as a coconut tree," Daniel said.

"Then where do coconuts come fr—" Joy stopped suddenly. "Whoa. Look under the trees."

Daniel shaded his eyes and spotted three hammocks and a firepit where Joy was pointing. The little shaded area looked comfy and inviting, the kind of place where a sea captain might relax after a long trip.

"So we're not alone," Daniel said.

"I guess not. Maybe we—" Joy said when Daniel

clutched his chest.

"My coat!"

"What coat? Your coat's gone."

"Exactly! So is yours. What happened? Where'd they go?"

"We just shot across the world to a tropical island," Joy told him. "Losing our winter clothes isn't our biggest concern."

Daniel touched his neck and felt a leather cord. "I'm wearing some kind of necklace. Oh! You're wearing one too."

"Cool." Joy fiddled with the blue bead on her necklace. "Where do you think these came from?"

"No idea. Add that to the bottom of our list of concerns."

"What's at the top?" she asked.

"Finding our way home, of course!"

"We can ask someone once we get over to that beach," Joy said.

Daniel eyed the empty beach. "What if the locals aren't friendly?"

"There are hammocks. Hammocks are *always* friendly. Plus, how else are we going to get home?"

Daniel nodded. "That's true."

"And I'm thirsty. Let's go drink from the coconuts." Joy tugged at his arm. "C'mon, race you to the hammocks!"

She started down the side of boulder toward the beach, then stopped short.

A second later, Daniel realized why: the white sandy shore didn't reach all the way to the boulder. Instead, a field of glistening mud stretched between him and Joy and the beach with the hammocks. The thick black mud, dotted with barnacle-encrusted stones and heaps of seaweed, gleamed beneath a few inches of water.

"Yuck," Joy said. "We're going to have walk through *that* to get to the beach?"

Daniel opened his mouth to answer, when—*SPLASH!* A slap of cold water splattered his face and arms.

He shouted in surprise, and Joy yelped. Then they looked at each other and cracked up.

"It's just a wave," Daniel said, as the water sloshed around the boulder.

But a few seconds later, prickles of sweat rose on his

neck. Not from the warm day though. From how the water was swirling over the muddy field that stretched between them and the beach.

"That *wasn't* just a wave," he said, his heart sinking. "That was the tide."

Joy bit her lower lip. "It's rising."

"And when it gets high enough," Daniel said, "we'll be stuck on this boulder."

"Not me!" Joy scrambled down toward the water. "I'm out of here."

"Wait!" Daniel called. "Hold on! Let's stay here and—"

"We can't stay here! There's nothing to eat or drink. We'll starve! Plus, there's a tropical island right over there! With *hammocks*!"

"Yeah, but you don't need to always rush into everything."

"Stop worrying," Joy told him, jumping the last few feet toward the water-covered mud. "This is nothing."

Except when she splashed down, she sunk into the mud. First to her ankles, then almost to her knees.

"Help!" Joy yelled. "This is *something*! It's quicksand! I'm sinking!"

"Pull her out!" a voice shouted from behind Daniel.

Chapter 3

Daniel spun around to see a girl about their age running toward them from the top of the boulder. For a second, he was so surprised at her sudden appearance that he just stared. Her ponytail bobbed and he caught a glimpse of the words on her T-shirt: *Don't Make Me SHUSH You!*

"Who are—" Daniel began, but the mystery girl cut him off.

"Hurry!" she yelled, trotting up behind him. "Before she sinks!"

"Yes!" Joy cried, as the mud reached her knees. "Hurrying would be good!"

Daniel clambered to the edge of the boulder. He gripped a stony ledge with one hand and reached for Joy's hand with his other.

"I've got you," he said, grabbing Joy's wrist.

"Pull me up!"

He gritted his teeth and pulled, but his hand slipped on the stone. Instead of pulling Joy out of the mud, he was pulling himself in!

"I can't!" he said. "I can't get a grip."

"Hold onto me," the new girl said, reaching out to Daniel.

Daniel took her hand. "Okay. You pull me and I'll pull Joy."

"On three," the new girl said. "One, two, THREE!"

The girl pulled Daniel's hand and he pulled Joy's wrist. For a second, nothing happened and Daniel's heart pounded with fear.

Then, all at once, Joy's legs un-splooshed from the

mud. Daniel and the mystery girl fell backwards as Joy flopped up onto the boulder.

"Wow." Joy looked at her muddy feet. "Yuck."

"Are you okay?" Daniel asked.

"Yeah." She brushed a strand of hair out of her face with a muddy hand. "The good news is, I learned one way that doesn't work."

"Huh?" the new girl asked, looking at them from above.

"Her dad taught her that," Daniel answered. "She says it whenever things don't go as planned."

"Which is pretty often," Joy admitted, wiping the muck from her legs.

"Because Joy's the kind of person who jumps into quicksand." Daniel squinted up at the girl. "Um, who are you? Do you know what's going on?"

"I'm Kimani," the girl said, then shook her head. "And I don't have a clue. I don't know where we are or how I got here or *anything*."

"We'll figure it out!" Joy said. "I'm Joy and this is my cousin, Daniel."

"Nice to meet you," Kimani said. "And I guess you're right. At least now we know that we can't walk across the mud. And the water's not deep enough to swim. Not yet anyway."

"We can't fly either," Joy said, climbing up the boulder toward Daniel. "I learned that the hard way, in first grade."

"She had a cape she thought was magic," Daniel explained.

"Because it *said* 'magic' on it," Joy said.

"Spelled M-A-J-I-K," Daniel said. "In glitter. After you painted it there."

"Anyway," Joy said, wrinkling her nose at him. "I guess if none of us knows anything, then we're all in the same boat. Or, um, on the same tropical island."

"Except we're not *on* the island," Daniel said. "And there's quicksand between us and the beach."

"Ooh, there are hammocks and coconut trees," Kimani said, peering toward the island.

"Told you so," Joy said to Daniel.

"They still look like palm trees to me," Daniel said.

"They're coconut palms," Kimani explained. "Some palm trees grow coconuts, some grow dates, and some don't grow anything."

"Whoa," Joy said. "You know a lot about trees."

"I like to read."

"I like video games," Daniel said.

"And I like winter sports," Joy said.

"Making snowwomen is not a winter sport," Daniel said.

"Well, it isn't a *summer* sport."

"Wait," Kimani said. "So how did you two get here?"

"We were messing around in the snow," Daniel started to tell her, "when suddenly we heard drums. Coming from all around us."

"Not at first," Joy said. "First we heard cars going *whap-pap-badabap* in the street."

"Yeah." Daniel ran his fingers through his hair. "We started drumming along, then the world turned inside out and *poof*. Here we were. How about you?"

"Same thing, except I was in the library."

"What were you doing there?" Joy asked.

"Um… reading?" Kimani fiddled with her ponytail. "What do *you* do at the library?"

"No, I mean, were you doing anything *else*?"

"Let's see. I had my notebook open," she answered, holding up a small spiral-bound pad.

"Whoa," Joy interrupted. "Cool. What do you use a notebook for?"

"Taking notes," Kimani said.

Daniel snorted a laugh. "What Joy means is, were you drumming your fingers? Humming a tune?"

"Oh! Well, I might've been tapping my pencil on my notebook. I do that a lot."

"Tapping is like drumming," Joy said.

"True," Kimani said. "Hm. What were you two thinking about right before it happened?"

Daniel tried to remember. "I was wishing that school was as fun as vacation."

"Me too!" Joy said. "I was thinking that too!"

"I was probably wishing that real life was as exciting as books," Kimani said, her eyes brightening. "Then I heard drumming, which doesn't happen much in a library."

"It does if Joy's around," Daniel said.

"The drumming got louder and faster," Kimani said, "until the whole building disappeared and I ended up here."

"Hey! You have a necklace too," Daniel said, spotting a leather cord around her neck.

"I know." Kimani touched the blue bead on her necklace. "But I don't know how I got it. None of this makes any sense."

"There's only one logical explanation," Joy said.

"What's that?" Kimani asked.

"Magic!" she answered.

Chapter 4

"**M**agic isn't logical," Daniel said.

"Yeah," Kimani said. "But we need to think logically if we're going to get off this boulder. The mud's too quicksand-y to wade to the island and the tide's too low to swim there. Although..."

"What?" Daniel asked.

Kimani pointed at the stone outcropping rising from the top of the boulder like a chimney. "I don't know what logical explanation there is for *that*."

"That's just part of this ginormous boulder," Joy said, then widened her eyes. "Oh! You mean those poles?"

When Daniel followed her gaze, he saw dozens of poles leaning against the outcropping, most of them taller than he was.

"Is that bamboo?" he asked.

"Looks like it," Kimani said. "But I'm not talking about the poles. I'm talking about the trunk."

A wooden chest was half-hidden in the shade behind the poles. And even though it looked a thousand years old, the symbol painted on top of it was bright and fresh: a circle filled with colored stars.

"Is that a trunk?" Daniel said.

Joy whooped. "It's a treasure chest!"

"What's inside?" Daniel asked Kimani.

"How would I know?"

"*Treasure*, obviously," Joy said, racing toward it. "That's why it's called a treasure chest. I bet it's full of rubies and diamonds and doubloons."

"What are doubloons?" Daniel asked, as he and Kimani followed her.

"They're like loons, but twice as valuable. Double-loon."

Kimani laughed. "Actually, doubloons are gold coins that were made by the Spanish hundreds of years ago."

"So definitely worth more than plain old loons," Joy said. She threw the lid of the chest open, then frowned. "It's full of bridges."

"Huh?" Daniel asked, stepping beside her.

"Well, pictures of bridges anyway." Joy wrinkled her nose. "And no gold coins at all."

Daniel looked at the sketches piled in the trunk. Each one seemed to show a different bridge. "That's weird."

"And not even worth *half* a loon," Joy grumbled, grabbing a sketch off the pile.

"That's Sydney Harbor," Kimani said, looking over Joy's shoulder.

"Never heard of him," Joy said.

"Sydney's not a person," Kimani said. "It's a city in Australia. And the Sydney Harbor Bridge is in the harbor there."

Daniel looked at the picture, which showed a metal arch made up of triangular sections. He turned to the rest of the sketches. "Do you recognize any others?"

"This one is Tower Bridge," Kimani said, tapping another sketch. "In London."

In the sketch, the bridge's two square towers were connected to each other by a road on the lower level and walkways on the upper level. The outsides of the towers had swooping cables, also made up of triangular sections, linking them to land.

Joy stuck her head in the trunk. "There's a bunch of toothpicks under the sketches," she said, her voice muffled. "And—ew. A block of mud."

Daniel squeezed in closer to his cousin. "Toothpicks and mud?"

"Well, the mud looks more like clay," she said. "And the toothpicks are bamboo twigs."

"I think this is Pearl Bridge in Japan," Kimani said, flipping through the sketches. "It's the longest suspension bridge in the world."

"How do you know so much about bridges?" Daniel asked her.

Before Kimani could answer, Joy said, "Look! There's a poem!" Daniel pulled a sheet of paper from the chest and read aloud:

One path is safe for your brave band,
Two lengths of tide you all must span,
Three sides will lead you to dry land.

"What does that mean?" Joy asked. "It doesn't make any sense."

"Unless..." Kimani squinted at the paper. "...*we're* the 'brave band.'"

"So we have to cross two lengths of tide to reach the beach?" Joy asked.

Kimani nodded. "Whoever brought us here must've left this as a riddle or instructions or—" She stopped as another wave slapped the base of the boulder. "Look! The tide's coming in faster."

"Yeah." Daniel ran his fingers through his hair. "How are we going to cross that mud?"

"We could wait for the tide to come in and then swim," Joy suggested.

"Without a lifeguard?" Daniel said. "Aren't there deadly currents in places like this?"

Joy dug into the chest. "Maybe there's something in here we can use."

"Sure," Daniel said. "Like a big stack of life jackets."

"Or a pitcher of lemonade," Joy said. "I'm thirsty."

"We might have another problem," Kimani said, staring at the muddy field between the boulder and the beach. "I just remembered a book I read."

"About what?" Daniel asked.

"Sharks," Kimani said, biting her lower lip. "They often live in warm water near the shore."

"Um…" Daniel fiddled with the leather cord of his necklace. "*This* is warm water near the shore."

"Exactly," Kimani said.

"So we're not just stranded on a ginormous boulder in some other dimension," Daniel said. "We're also fish food!"

Chapter 5

"**S**peak for yourself, I'm not going to be shark bait!" Joy said. "I'm working on a plan."

Daniel turned to her. "What plan?"

"Well, step three is napping in one of those hammocks," Joy said, pointing to the island. "Step two is landing safely on the beach."

"What's step one?"

"I'm still working on that part."

He snorted. "You know what you are?"

"A shipwreck," Kimani said.

"I wouldn't call her a 'shipwreck'!" Daniel said. "She's

not that bad. I was thinking more like 'potato-head.'"

Joy slugged Daniel's arm. "Hey!"

"I'm not talking about Joy," Kimani said. "I'm talking about an actual shipwreck! C'mon!"

She led them around the outcropping and pointed in the one direction they hadn't looked yet. Thick, barnacle-covered beams poked out of the mud twenty or thirty feet away, surrounding what looked like a log cabin after a mudslide.

When Daniel shaded his eyes, he saw that the rotten beams were the half-buried hull of an old wooden ship, stuck in the mud between them and the beach.

"Whoa," he said. "That really is a shipwreck."

"Who's the potato-head now?" Joy asked.

"It must've run aground a long time ago," Kimani said.

"Probably chased by sharks," Daniel muttered.

"I bet it was a pirate ship!" Joy said. "Maybe it's full of treasure!"

"Maybe it's our way to the beach," Kimani said.

"How?" Daniel asked. "It's too far to jump to."

"Look there." Kimani pointed to a low, flat rock in the muddy field between them and the shipwreck. "The poem said, 'Two lengths of tide,' remember? If we can get from this boulder to that flat rock, then from the rock to the shipwreck, we can reach the beach in two stages. That's our path to safety."

Daniel nodded. The closer end of the wrecked wooden ship was in the mud, but the farther end was in the white sand of the island. It looked like an easy jump from the far side of the shipwreck to the beach. That way they could avoid the mud entirely.

"That will totally work," he said.

"See?" Joy told Daniel. "That's step one. Now my plan is complete!"

Daniel ignored her, looking at the muddy field. The flat rock was about ten feet from the ginormous boulder, and the shipwreck was about ten or fifteen feet beyond that.

"They're like stepping stones," he said.

"Except we can't step," Kimani said. "They're too far from each other."

"Not if we jump," Joy said, and backed up to get a running start.

"Wait!" Daniel grabbed her arm. "If you miss, you'll end up neck deep in the mud."

"Which is *exactly* why I won't miss."

"Remember that time you jumped from the climbing wall to the balance beam?"

"I almost made it!"

"You got seven stitches."

"Okay." Joy sighed. "Maybe jumping isn't the best idea. But what else can we do?"

For a moment, nobody spoke.

Then Kimani laughed. "The bridges! The bridges in the trunk!"

Daniel smiled. "Of course!"

"Yes, of course! Obviously!" Joy cried. "Wait. Of course *what*?"

"The pictures in the treasure chest are another clue," Daniel told her. "We need to build bridges to get to the beach."

"Okay, but how do we—" Joy snapped her fingers. "The

bamboo! We can build bridges out of bamboo."

They each dragged a bamboo pole across the boulder, closer to the flat rock. Joy stretched her pole through the air toward the rock, but the far end plopped into the mud a few feet short. She grumbled, then Kimani tried. Her pole came closer, but still didn't quite make it.

Then Daniel lifted his bamboo pole over the muck toward the rock. The farther he extended the pole, the

heavier it felt. He stretched and stretched, his arms trembling. He grunted with effort, until finally the far end of the bamboo touched down on the edge of the rock.

"Awesome!" Joy said.

"Good job!" Kimani said.

"Pretty!" a shrill voice called.

Daniel yelped in surprise as a yellow-and-blue blur swooped down from above.

"Hey!" Joy shouted.

"Wha—?" Daniel started, when the blur landed on his shoulder.

"A parrot," Kimani said, with a smile. "It's a parrot!"

"Pretty!" the parrot repeated, rubbing Daniel's head with its beak.

The bird's sharp claws poked through Daniel's shirt, but he didn't care. His heart beat fast and he felt himself smiling along with Kimani. A parrot had flown over from the island and landed right on his shoulder!

The parrot had a yellow body with blue wings, and a green patch on top of its head. It also had a blue dot on its throat. Except it wasn't a dot.

Daniel gasped. "It's wearing a necklace! Just like ours!"

"He!" the bird squawked, cocking its head. "He!"

"O-kay," Daniel said, slowly. "*He's* wearing a necklace just like ours."

"You're pretty!" the bird told Daniel.

Daniel laughed. "No way!"

"Way!" the parrot said.

"Did he just say 'way'?" Daniel asked.

"He totally did." Joy reached out to stroke the parrot's back. "Ooh! His feathers are soft as... as feathers! What should we call him?"

"DaVinci!" the parrot squawked. "DaVinci!"

"DaVinci?" Daniel said.

"That must be his name," Kimani told him. "Parrots are smart that way."

"Way!" DaVinci said.

Daniel laughed again.

"Ahoy, matey!" DaVinci called as he launched himself off Daniel's shoulder and flew back toward the beach.

"Wow," Kimani said.

"Yeah," Joy said, her eyes wide. "He's like a parrot pirate."

Daniel didn't say anything. He just watched DaVinci disappear into the trees.

"I wonder who gave him that necklace," Joy said. "And who gave us ours."

Kimani twirled her ponytail thoughtfully. "Maybe it's the same person who brought us here."

Chapter 6

"**N**ow I really have to get to the island!" Daniel said. "I want to see DaVinci again."

"And I want to get back home," Kimani said.

"So the rising tide isn't enough reason for you two?" Joy asked.

Daniel and Kimani didn't answer. They were too busy stretching more poles across to the low, flat rock. It was easier now that they could rest them on the pole that was already in place.

"Ta-da!" Daniel said, when he put the last pole across. "A bridge."

Five pieces of bamboo stretched from the ginormous boulder to the edge of the flat rock, like this:

"They're going to roll apart if we step on them," Joy said.

"I saw some vines on the other side of the boulder," Kimani said. "We can tie the poles together!"

Daniel glanced at Joy, and she smiled back. She knew a hundred knots, with wacky names like Monkey's Fist and Lariat Loop and Rolling Hitch. In the third grade she'd gotten them into trouble by teaching Daniel to tie Sheet Bend knots using their classmates' backpack straps. By the end of the day, twenty backpacks were tied together in one massive tangled knot.

They pulled the bamboo poles back onto the boulder. Then Daniel and Kimani brought armloads of vines to Joy and watched her tie the poles together.

"C'mere, I'll show you how," Joy said, and handed each

of them a vine. "This one's called a Square Lashing. You start here, then loop it around like this."

As they sat in the sun, listening to the surf and tying knots, Daniel almost forgot about the rising tide. First, because he kept thinking about DaVinci. He'd never seen a parrot before—much less had one land on his shoulder! And second, because one of the things he liked most about sports was teamwork. Everyone helping each other out. The knot tying gave him the same feeling.

In no time at all, Daniel, Joy, and Kimani tied the five bamboo poles together into a makeshift bridge.

"Much better," Daniel said.

Working together, they lifted the walkway over the muddy ground. Then they lowered the far end from the ginormous boulder onto the low, flat rock.

"It reaches!" Kimani said, wiping sweat from her forehead.

Daniel looked from the bridge to Kimani. "Yeah, but who crosses first?"

"You're the biggest," Kimani said. "If it'll hold you, it'll hold us. But going first is scary, so—"

"It's working!" Joy cried.

Daniel turned and saw her standing out on the walkway, a few feet out over the mud. She was hopping up and down.

Kimani blinked. "Oh. Never mind."

"Yeah," Daniel said. "Joy isn't afraid of scary."

Joy spread her arms, balancing on the wobbly walkway, a couple feet above the mud and rising tide. She took one step, then another.

The walkway bowed lower and lower... then stopped six inches above the muck. A few seconds later, Joy reached the flat-topped rock. The bamboo poles had separated a little on that side, so she took some vines that she'd draped around her neck and tied them together.

"C'mon!" she called. "The tide's still rising."

Kimani went next. She stepped onto the bridge and

wobbled toward Joy.

"Looking good!" Daniel told her.

When Kimani reached the low, flat rock, she waved to Daniel. "It's actually kind of fun!"

"I can already taste the coconuts," Joy said.

Daniel shot her a grin as he stepped onto the bridge. It felt like walking on five balance beams pressed together, except these beams were round and slippery. Still, he'd always been good at the balance beam. He walked onto the bridge with no problem.

CREAK!

Oh no! The bamboo started to bend under his weight. His breath caught and he froze.

"Keep going," Kimani urged him. "You're doing great."

"And you're looking tasty," Joy said. "At least to any sharks who might be nearby."

That got him moving again. He took another step, and another. When he reached the middle of the bridge, the bamboo bent so low it almost touched the water. The vine knots stretched and creaked.

Daniel inched forward, his heart pounding. Another full step and—

CRACK!

The bamboo jerked under his feet.

Joy screamed, "RUN!"

Chapter 7

Daniel ran.

The walkway swayed and bounced wildly. His feet slipped on the wet bamboo. He lurched and almost fell. But he caught his balance and pounded forward. A few feet from the end, he flung himself onto the low, flat rock.

Joy grabbed him and helped him up. Daniel leaned over, his hands on his knees, breathing hard.

"Please tell me," he panted, "that the next gap is shorter."

"The next gap is shorter," Joy said.

"Good," Daniel said, closing his eyes and listening to the tide lap at the sides of the flat rock.

"Actually," Kimani said, "it's farther from here to the shipwreck."

"Yeah," Joy said.

Daniel's eyes sprung open. "Then why'd you say it was shorter?"

"You told me to! You even said 'please.'"

"We just have to build a stronger bridge this time," Kimani said. "One that'll hold our weight better."

"One that'll hold *Daniel's* weight," Joy said, elbowing him. "Small people rule."

"Funny how you never complain about my size when you need a boost up into a tree," he said.

"Details, details," Joy said, then stomped her foot on the low, flat rock. "I hereby claim this as Joylandia!"

Daniel eyed the wet, slimy stone they were standing on. It was as flat as his kitchen table, and only just a little bigger. And totally empty.

"Well, there's nothing on Joylandia," he said, "that will

help us build a stronger bridge or—hey!"

Water splashed his ankles and soaked his sneakers. A few of the highest waves were already lapping across the top of the flat rock.

"Whatever we do," he told Kimani, "we'd better do it fast."

"Why are you looking at me?" Kimani asked.

"Because you *know* things." An idea popped into his head. "Hey, do you think we were chosen to come here because we have different strengths?"

"What do you mean?"

"Well, you're good with knowing things. Joy is good at taking risks."

"And what are *you* good at?" Kimani asked.

"Parrots?" he said, with a shrug.

Joy snorted. "You're steady."

"What does that mean?" he asked.

"You're good at knowing when *not* to take risks," she explained.

Daniel had been hoping for something cooler than

that, but he said, "Yeah, I guess. It's like we were picked to be a team together."

"Then let's think this through... together." Kimani looked out at the ocean and repeated the poem.

> *One path is safe for your brave band,*
> *Two lengths of tide you all must span,*
> *Three sides will lead you to dry land.*

"So we're half done already," Daniel said. "We crossed one length of tide. One more length of tide and we'll reach the shipwreck. From there, we can just climb down to the beach."

"But three sides?" Kimani wiped her hands on her T-shirt. "What does that part mean?"

"Maybe there's another clue in the chest," Joy said.

"I bet everything in that chest is a clue," Daniel said. "Or a tool."

"Oh!" Kimani said. "Maybe we need to use the twigs and clay."

"Say no more," Joy said, trotting back across the walkway. When she reached the ginormous boulder, she yelled, "Don't go anywhere!"

"Where could we possibly go?" Kimani asked Daniel.

He grinned. "Yeah, like we might sneak off to the movies without her."

"I wish we could go bowling," Kimani said. "I love bowling."

"*Never* bowl with Joy," he said with a shudder. "She doesn't understand the concept of 'staying in your own lane.'"

Kimani giggled.

"So, uh, what are we going to do with bamboo twigs and clay?" Daniel asked.

"Make a little bridge," Kimani told him.

"What, so Joy can scamper across? She's small enough."

"I heard that!" Joy yelled, from the boulder.

"No, like a scale model," Kimani told Daniel.

"What good will that do?" Daniel asked, stepping to the center of Joylandia. The tide was rising up over the edges and splashed onto the rock.

"It will show us how to build the strongest bridge possible. We can't waste time making one that doesn't work," Kimani said.

Joy returned with the brick of clay and bamboo twigs bulging from her pockets, plus some extra bamboo poles over her shoulder.

"So what now?" Daniel asked.

Kimani took the clay from Joy and rolled a chunk of it into a marble-sized ball. "Make a bunch of these."

He started shaping little balls. "What're they for?"

"Nothing," she said. "I just like making them."

"*What*?"

Kimani laughed. "I'm kidding! We'll use them to connect the twigs together."

After they'd made a bunch of balls, Kimani pushed two bamboo twigs into one, like this:

Then she added another ball of clay and another twig to make this:

"Make a bunch of those," she said.

After Daniel and Joy finished, Kimani connected the longer sticks to each other, like this:

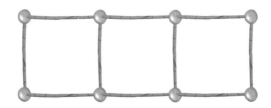

"Now we have a ladder," Joy said. "How does that help us?"

"It's not a ladder," Kimani said. "It's a bridge! This part is just the lower level. We have to make another one for the upper level."

"And then what?" Daniel asked.

"We connect them and test if it's stronger."

Daniel peered at the water swirling across Joylandia and over his shoes "We better test it *fast*," he said.

They made another ladder like the first one, then connected the two:

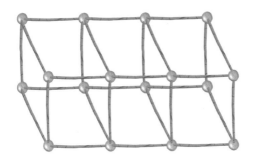

Kimani squeezed the model in her hands. "Yeah, a two-level bridge is way stronger than a single-level walkway."

A wave crashed, spraying water across the low rock. "I hope you're right," Daniel said.

"If not," Joy said, "we'll be three skeletons trapped in the quickmud."

"'Quickmud'?" Daniel asked.

"It's like quicksand," Joy explained, "but slimier."

"I don't care what it's called as long as we can get across it," Daniel said. "We're running out of time!"

Chapter 8

"We'll be okay," Kimani told them. "Daniel's right about us having different strengths. We're a team for a reason. And if we work together, we can do anything."

Daniel and Kimani sorted through the bamboo poles, giving the best ones to Joy, who tied them together with strong knots... while humming a silly tune.

"You're enjoying this!" Daniel said.

Joy grinned. "A little."

"We're trapped here, and the tide's almost to my ankles!"

"Sure, but you've got to admit you're not bored."

"That's true," Daniel said with a laugh. "And the

weather's great."

After Joy tied the last knot, she said, "Ta-da!"

"Pretty cool," Daniel said, eyeing the new bridge. "It looks just like Kimani's little scale model."

"Ahoy!" DaVinci called. "Ahoy!"

Daniel shaded his eyes and saw a colorful streak flashing down from the sky.

"DaVinci!" Daniel said, as the parrot landed on his shoulder. "You came back!"

"Look what he brought!" Kimani said, her voice bright with excitement.

DaVinci was holding a bundle of tropical flowers in his beak. There was a blue ribbon tied around the stems.

As Daniel patted one of DaVinci's scaly talons, the parrot shook his head and scattered the flowers across the ground. All but one. Then he flew to a strut of the bridge, and jabbed the last flower into one of the knots.

"I don't believe it! Your parrot is decorating the bridge," Kimani said.

"Wasn't Leonardo da Vinci an artist?" Daniel asked.

"Maybe the parrot's named DaVinci because he likes to decorate things."

"Leonardo da Vinci was a scientist too," Kamini said. "And an architect. So *this* DaVinci is helping us be like *that* da Vinci!"

"Pretty, pretty!" DaVinci said. "Walk the plank!"

"Whoa," Joy said, rummaging among the flowers on the ground. "Please tell me that you heard that too."

"Yeah," Daniel said, as he added a few more flowers to the bridge. "He sounds more like a pirate than an architect!"

"I think he's a macaw," Kimani said. "They're really smart. I read they can learn to say whole sentences."

"Parrot!" DaVinci replied. "Pretty parrot!"

"Macaws *are* parrots," Kimani said, as if she was afraid she'd offended him.

"Walk the plank!" DaVinci repeated, flapping back to the bridge.

Daniel said, "I think he's calling our bridge a plank."

"Ahoy!" DaVinci took flight, circled Joylandia twice,

then landed on Daniel's shoulder again.

"DaVinci, where did you get this?" Daniel asked, touching the necklace around the bird's throat.

DaVinci cocked his head and said, "Boom-baDOOM-boom-boom-badoom!"

"The drums!" Kimani blurted. "That's the drumming I heard!"

"Us too!" Joy said to the parrot. "We heard the same thing."

"Boom," DaVinci said, then launched himself from Daniel's shoulder. A few moments later he disappeared over the island treetops in a swirl of color.

Kimani looked at the flower-draped bridge. "Well, DaVinci's right about one thing. It is prettier now."

"So am I!" Joy announced. "Look!"

Daniel smiled when he saw that she was wearing the blue ribbon as a headband. "Nice," he said.

"We should all wear headbands," Joy said. "Because we're a team."

"There's only one ribbon," Kimani said.

"We'll take turns," Joy said.

"Let's worry about getting to the island first," Daniel said, pressing down on the bridge. "Oh, it's definitely stronger now."

"And more beautiful with the flowers added," said Joy.

"That's art and science working together!" Kimani thought for a second, twisting her ponytail. "But I still don't see what 'three sides' means in that poem."

"Doesn't matter," Joy said. "Let's get moving."

They swung the bridge into place. Daniel's back ached and his hands burned, but the three of them managed to drop the far end of the bridge onto the edge of the shipwreck.

"Daniel should go first this time," Joy said. "That way if he can't get across, he won't be stuck here by himself."

"And we'll know it can hold us," Kimani added.

So Daniel stepped onto the bridge. "Here goes nothing," he said. He took a step and the bamboo poles felt steady under his feet. He took two more steps, and smiled. No problem. Easy pea—

CREAK!

Suddenly, the bamboo poles jerked beneath his feet. Daniel heard a cracking noise. It sounded like the poles were splintering from the inside.

Daniel froze.

Chapter 9

Daniel was sure that if he took one more step, the bridge would snap. He tried not to think about falling into quickmud and being stuck there while the ocean tide covered him.

He held his breath, listening for another creak. Faint crackles sounded from the bamboo under his feet.

"It's okay," Joy called. "Keep going."

"It won't hold me!" he told her. "You two use the bridge. I'll swim across once the tide rises."

"What if it doesn't get high enough to swim?" Kimani said. "You'll get stuck."

"It's worth a try," he said.

"No, it's not." Joy pointed at the ocean. "Look!"

The water rippled around the base of the ginormous boulder they'd started on. And not far past it, a shiny, curved fin rose from the surf, then vanished.

"Shark!" Daniel yelled, his blood freezing. "Shark!"

"Maybe that's not a shark fin. Maybe it's a—a something else!" Kimani said, talking fast, like she was nervous. "Or maybe, maybe the shark is more afraid of you than you are of it!"

"It's *not* more afraid of me!" Daniel hollered at her. "I am definitely more afraid of the shark."

CREAK! The bridge jerked under him again.

"Come back!" Joy bellowed. "Run!"

Daniel ran.

Sharks! His heart pounded in his chest, fast as a drumroll, as his mind screamed. *Sharks, sharks, sharks...*

As he raced back toward Kimani and Joy, the bridge swayed and shook. His vision narrowed and—

CRACK!

One bamboo pole snapped an instant after his sneaker shoved off it.

He yelped, but kept running. Even faster. And then, two steps from the flat-topped rock of Joylandia, he lost his balance.

He toppled off the bridge and splashed into the ocean.

The cool water felt like shark's teeth on his legs, and when he stood up the quickmud sucked at his feet.

He gasped and lunged for the flat rock. The mud gripped him tightly until Joy grabbed one arm and Kimani the other. They dragged him free of the muck and up onto Joylandia.

"Are you okay?" Joy asked, giving his arm a squeeze.

Daniel nodded, breathing heavily, then collapsed in the middle of the flat rock while Kimani heaved the broken bridge beside him.

The three of them sat in silence, watching the ocean. Every now and then, a curved fin broke the surface.

"Okay," Kimani said. "Let's forget the sharks for now."

"I will never, *ever* forget the sharks," Daniel told her.

"We need to focus on reaching that shipwreck," Kimani said, turning toward the island. "From the other end of the wreck, we can hop onto the beach."

"But our bridge wasn't strong enough to hold Daniel," Joy said. "And the poem said, 'Two lengths of tide you *all* must span.'"

Daniel made a face at her. "I'm glad there's one reason not to leave me here."

"There are two." Kimani lightly kicked one of his muddy shoes. "We're a team, right?"

"Wait a second," Joy said, fiddling with her blue headband. "Maybe *we're* the three sides."

"We're not really sides though," Kimani said.

"Oh. Yeah."

"What has three sides?"

"A shark's tooth," Daniel said, eyeing the ocean.

"Shark's teeth are cool," Kimani said. "Did you know that you can estimate the size of a shark by measuring one of its teeth?"

"I do *not* want to talk about sharks right now!" Daniel

snapped, even though he was the one who had brought it up in the first place.

"A slice of pizza is triangular," Joy said, changing the subject.

"Some sails are triangular," Kimani said.

Another wave splashed Daniel, and he realized that a few inches of water now covered Joylandia.

He shivered and stared at the shipwreck.

It looked like it must've run aground hundreds of years ago. Barnacle-covered beams stretched across the remains of rotting planks. The few flat areas—floors or walls, he couldn't tell—were black and slimy from the sea. Still, the other side of the decaying ship was half-buried in solid sand, away from the quickmud. If they made it to the shipwreck, they could easily reach the beach from there.

They could lounge in the hammocks, drink from the coconuts, and... what? And find whoever brought them here—and demand to go home.

Daniel sighed. Except they couldn't get to the shipwreck.

All they had was a half-broken bridge, a chunk of clay, and some bamboo twigs. And a hungry shark with a mouth full of teeth...

"Triangular teeth," he muttered, as an idea formed in his mind.

"Huh?" Joy said.

"Triangles!" he told her. "Like in the pictures. The *bridges!*"

Kimani gave a sudden laugh. "You're right! Triangles!"

"Circles!" Joy said. "Rectangles!"

Daniel peered at her. "What are *you* talking about?"

"Aren't we listing shapes?" Joy asked.

"No, look!" Kimani pulled out the sketches she'd tucked into her pocket earlier. "London Bridge, Sydney Harbor Bridge, Pearl Bridge. What do they all have in common?"

Joy stared at the sketches. She squinted. She scratched her nose and tapped her feet.

Then she laughed.

Chapter 10

"Triangles!" Joy yelled. "The bridges are all made up of smaller, triangle shapes."

"Exactly!" Kimani said. "We need to make a bridge with triangles in it."

"Let me guess," Daniel said. "Time for another model?"

Kimani rummaged in her pockets and pulled out the bamboo twigs and clay. Then she made this:

"Check it out," she said, handing the model to Daniel.

He squeezed it, but the twigs barely moved. "Wow. It's way stronger now."

"There's just one problem," Joy said.

"What?" he asked.

Joy pointed. "We don't have enough bamboo to build a new bridge. All that's left are these short pieces. They aren't even long enough to reach the shipwreck."

Kimani took her model back. She looked toward the island chain in the distance.

Nobody spoke as a wave sloshed across Joylandia then rolled over the muddy field and splashed the shipwreck.

Finally, Kimani said, "I've got it! We'll turn each square of the old bridge into two triangles. We'll add diagonal pieces, and turn this..."

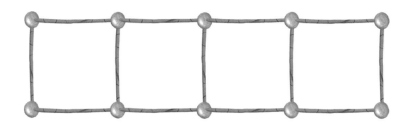

"...into *this*!"

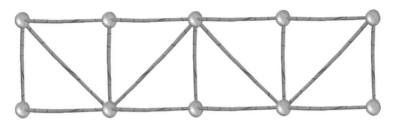

"Turn four squares into eight triangles," Daniel said, shaking his head in awe. "Now *that* is magic."

The tide swirled around Daniel's ankles as Joy tied diagonal pieces across the rectangular sections of the bridge. When she finished, Daniel pressed on the top level, and the bamboo poles barely shifted.

"I think this is called a truss bridge," Kimani said. "I hope it works."

"I'm not worried," Joy told her. "I totally *truss* you."

Daniel groaned and Kimani laughed—then a big wave splashed them, and they got moving. They hefted the bridge hand-over-hand through the air. The truss bridge was so strong that it barely drooped, and a minute later it stretched over the mud, linking

Joylandia to the shipwreck.

"Now we're talking," Daniel said.

"Time to stop talking and get moving!" Joy said.

When Daniel climbed onto the truss bridge, it felt strong and stable. The bamboo barely bent at all under his weight. He took a moment to check the water, but didn't see any fins. So he squared his shoulders and took a step out over the mud. Then another and another.

In the middle of the bridge, halfway to the shipwreck, the bamboo poles sagged a little—but not much.

Daniel kept moving, and reached the end of the bridge. He climbed onto the shipwreck like it was a jungle gym made of rotting planks and shouted, "Safe!"

"Hooray!" Joy cheered.

Daniel gave a bow, then waited for them to join him.

"You go next," Joy told Kimani, and—

SPLASH! A wave hit the truss bridge, which jerked and started sliding toward the water.

On the shipwreck, Daniel grabbed the nearest pole of the bamboo bridge. It bucked in his hands, but he held on

tight. On the flat rock, Joy and Kimani clung to their end
of the bridge until the wave passed.

"C'mon!" Daniel called. "Move!"

Joy nudged Kimani onto the bridge. "Go!"

Kimani walked quickly across, the ocean just inches
below her feet. Another wave sloshed against the bridge,
but Daniel and Joy held tightly onto each end until
Kimani climbed safely onto the shipwreck.

"Hurry!" Daniel called to Joy.

Joy jumped onto the bridge and started running.

When she was halfway across, a third wave slammed
the bridge right behind her. With no one holding it, the
far end of the bridge slid off Joylandia and splashed into
the ocean.

Joy fell.

Daniel gasped, his heart clenching.

With a yelp, Joy caught hold of the bridge. She hefted
herself onto it and balanced on all fours. As she crawled
closer, Daniel reached for her. Kimani grunted behind

him, holding the bridge steady as the far end bobbed in the waves.

Finally, Joy was close enough for Daniel to grab her hand. The instant he did, another wave smashed into the bridge. It jerked away with the wave as Daniel yanked Joy onto the shipwreck... and into *him*.

He stumbled backward and slammed against a slanting wall of wooden planks.

"Oof!" he said.

"That was awesome!" Joy said, her eyes shining below her headband.

"Except that last part," Daniel groaned.

Joy peered at the broken pieces of bamboo floating in water. "Thank you for helping us, Bridge," she called out. "You were very brave!"

"*We* were very brave!" Kimani said with a laugh.

"Bravery makes me thirsty," Joy said.

"We can drink coconut water once we get to the beach," Kimani said.

"Yeah, while swinging in hammocks!"

"We're not looking for coconuts or hammocks," Daniel reminded them, leaning against the weather-beaten wall and catching his breath. "We're looking for a way home! And maybe a parrot."

"Hm." Joy looked to Kimani. "Do you know if pirates are into playing the drums?"

"This might not be a pirate ship," Kimani told her.

"We need to—" Daniel started to say, when the wall moved behind him. "Yaiii!"

He spun around to see a long crack had opened right where he'd been leaning. The planks of the wall were gray with age, twisted and rotting... but this crack was perfectly straight. And spreading wider every second.

"It's a door," Kimani said, wonder in her voice. "You must've knocked it loose. Maybe it leads into the captain's quarters."

"The *pirate* captain's quarters, you mean," Joy said.

Daniel frowned at the dark space behind the cracked-open door. "Maybe we should—"

"Explore!" Joy announced.

She pushed past Daniel and through the doorway, disappearing into the darkness.

"Well, I did wish for some excitement," Kimani said.

"But *I* wished for fun!" Daniel joked.

They laughed and followed Joy to the inside of the shipwreck.

Chapter 11

The room inside was tilted at a steep angle, the floor boards half-covered with sand. Seawater sloshed around Daniel's sneakers. He blinked a few times as his eyes got used to the darkness. The air was cool and stank of rotting fish.

He wrinkled his nose. "Shipwrecks smell like cat food."

"In anchovy sauce," Joy added.

"This room must've stretched all the way across the stern," Kimani said. "I think it *was* the captain's quarters. That is so cool."

Daniel didn't say anything. To him the room looked like

a wooden shack that had spent way too long underwater. The ceiling tilted downward at a sharp angle, reaching almost to the sand-covered floor. Seagrass grew along the bottom of the rotting walls, and seaweed twined around a pile of wood that might've once been a bed or table.

Other than that, the room was empty.

"Think about it," Kimani said. "Hundreds of years ago, this ship's captain lived *right here*. He read his maps right where we're standing. He guided his ship across uncharted seas, braving storms and pirates and all kinds of dangers."

"That..." Joy fell silent for a moment. "That is pretty amazing."

"Look!" Kimani said, pointing to the ceiling above her head.

Sunlight trickling through the open doorway shone on a familiar symbol painted on the wood: a circle filled with colored stars.

"Just like on the treasure chest," Joy said. "I wonder what else is in here."

As Joy wandered toward a dim corner, Kimani reached up and touched the symbol.

"The colors are so bright," Kimani said. "How can it look new when the rest of the ship looks like it's been rotting here for centuries?"

"At least now we know where the treasure chest came from," Joy said.

"Yeah," Daniel said. "So one thing makes more sense."

"It makes *less* sense!" Kimani told him. "What are pictures of modern bridges doing in an ancient chest? Plus the bamboo and clay. And—and how about parrots wearing necklaces? How does any of that make sense?"

"Oh," Daniel said. "Right."

"The biggest mystery is this," Joy said. "What happened to the doubloons?"

"I guess someone must've found the trunk," Daniel said, "and taken it to the boulder where—"

"Oh no!" Joy stared at the floor in the lowest corner of the room. "We're sinking."

Water was bubbling into the captain's quarters, and

for a second Daniel thought Joy was right. But then he realized it was just the tide rising around the shipwreck, seeping in through cracks and holes.

"We've got to get out of here," Daniel said.

Kimani gave the symbol on the ceiling one last look. "Yeah, we should—"

"Wait!" Joy called, from her corner. "There's another poem here!"

"But the tide's still coming in," Daniel said. "And we're almost to the beach. Let's not push our luck."

"We wouldn't have made it this far without the first poem," Joy reminded him. "And this room's been here a million years! It's not going to fall apart now."

"I don't know..." Daniel said.

"Just two more seconds," Joy urged him. "C'mon, check it out!"

"Fine!" Daniel said, and stepped forward for a look at the new poem.

The floorboards sagged under his feet. He ducked

his head beneath the tilted ceiling and saw a sheet of parchment tacked to a rotting wall.

"It's the same handwriting as the other one," Kimani said from beside him.

The seagrass on the floor swayed in the current, and little waves went *splish-splash* against the walls as Joy read the poem aloud:

> *You'll play the games,*
> *You'll face the trials,*
> *You'll meet the challenge,*
> *Of these magic isles.*

"Magic!" Joy said. "I knew it!"

She thumped the parchment happily with her palm... and the rotting wall moved suddenly, toppling toward her.

"Help!" Joy screamed as she scrambled backwards.

Daniel raised his arm to fend off the falling wall, but it didn't hit him. Instead, it jammed against a barnacle-covered beam and stopped an inch above his head.

His heart pounded. "Let's go before this whole place falls apart!"

"But there's more to the poem," Joy said. "I didn't read all the lines. Maybe it tells how to get back home."

"I'll check," Kimani told Daniel. "Hold the wall steady."

"Are you kidding?" he asked.

"You're good at steady, remember?" Kimani crouched under the half-fallen wall. "Don't let it fall on me!"

Daniel pressed both hands against the waterlogged wall, so if it started to collapse again then Kimani would have time to get out from under it.

"Can you read it?" Joy called to Kimani.

"It's dark. I have to get closer."

"Hurry! The water's rising," Daniel said between gritted teeth.

"A team!" Kimani answered.

"Huh?" Joy asked.

Kimani read:

> *A team you'll forge,*
> *Before you're through,*
> *You'll protect...*

"Protect what?" Daniel asked.

"I can't quite read the rest. The clam? The claim?"

"Kimani!" Daniel grunted. "Come on!"

"The *chain*!" she yelled back before reading the last few lines.

> *You'll protect the chain,*
> *From the fateful spew.*

"At least I think that's what it says," Kimani said.

"Great! Let's go!" Daniel growled, water swirling around his calves.

"One more second. I'm not sure about that last line!" Kimani said. "I should double-check—"

Then Joy pulled Kimani's arm, yanking her toward the door an instant before the wall came crashing down.

Chapter 12

Water exploded around Daniel, drenching his face and stinging his eyes. He couldn't see!

He almost panicked, but Kimani grabbed his hand. And with Joy leading the way, the three of them stumbled through the door and into the sudden brightness.

The air smelled fresh and pure, and the surf gave a rumbling purr, like a snoring lioness.

"That was way too close," Daniel said, leaning against a beam on the shipwreck.

"Don't worry," Joy told him. "We're safe as long as I'm wearing my lucky headband."

"What makes you think it's lucky?"

"Because we're safe. That proves it!"

He groaned at her, then turned to Kimani. "So are we the 'brave band' from the first poem and the 'team' from the second one? Are the poems about *us*?"

"Looks that way to me," Kimani said. "But what does 'protect the chain' mean?"

"And what's a spew?" Joy asked.

"Maybe they're metaphors," Kimani said. "It is a poem, after all."

"You mean some words in the poem have different meanings?" Daniel said. "Like 'chain' is actually something else?"

"What are we, back in school again?" Joy grumbled.

"I think it's interesting," Kimani said.

"You know what I think is interesting?" Joy said. "Tropical islands!" She took off running across the shipwreck, weaving through planks that stuck up like a whale's ribs. "Last one to the beach is a rotten coconut!" she called over her shoulder.

Kimani and Daniel watched for a second, then laughed and chased after her.

At the edge of the shipwreck facing the island, they stopped running and peered down. Through the shallow layer of water, the ground looked white and solid, not like quickmud.

Daniel said, "We should see how deep the water—"

SPLASH!

Joy had already jumped off the shipwreck.

She splashed through knee-deep water, wading safely toward the dry sand. Her feet didn't sink at all. "The water's warm!"

"And now," Daniel told Kimani, "we know one way that *does* work."

"C'mon," Joy called, smiling back at them.

Daniel and Kimani jumped down behind her, landing with a splash.

The three of them sloshed through the shallow water until they reached the beach. Shells dotted the sand and little birds ran from each incoming wave, leaving triangular tracks behind. The emerald jungle beyond the sand looked bright and welcoming. Colorful birds swooped and flashed among the branches and sang *eep-twee-diddee-ee.*

"Race you to the hammocks!" Joy yelled, sprinting ahead.

Daniel trotted after her, but slowed when he noticed two small black triangles lying on the beach among the pebbles.

"Arrowheads!" he yelled.

"Those aren't arrowheads." Kimani crouched beside him. "They're shark teeth. Fossilized shark teeth, actually. Those could be 10,000 years old."

Daniel scooped the black triangles into his hand. "No way."

"Way!" DaVinci called, landing on his shoulder again. "Way."

"Okay, okay," Daniel said, stroking the parrot's smooth neck. "They're shark teeth. I believe you."

"Shark teeth are really cool," Kimani said. "If you

measure a shark tooth in inches, then multiply by ten, you get the length of the shark in feet."

Daniel held up a tooth. "So this one-inch tooth came from a ten-foot shark?"

"Yep."

"Then it's definitely not from the sharks who were trying to eat me," Daniel said. "Those were at least sixty feet long."

"You weren't even close to getting eaten!" Kimani told him, and started rattling off shark facts.

The surf crashed, the wind ruffled the trees, and Daniel only half-listened to Kimani as they followed Joy's footsteps toward the ring of palm trees that rose over the hammocks and firepit.

"Did you know that great white sharks can detect electrical currents?" Kimani asked. "It helps them catch their—oh! Oh! Oh!"

"Catch their oh?" Daniel asked, eyeing Kimani as she hopped around the beach.

"Look, look!" Kimani pointed at the ocean. "Look!"

A dozen fins sliced through the waves, and for a moment Daniel's heart clenched. Then two dolphins jumped into sight. They leaped together in perfect curves, completely out of the water, then splashed down and disappeared.

From farther along the beach, Joy shouted, "Dolphins!"

"I told you they weren't sharks!" Kimani said, gazing in wonder toward the ocean.

"Maybe *those* weren't sharks," Daniel said, rattling the shark teeth in his palm. "But there are definitely sharks out there somewhere."

"Hard to port!" DaVinci squawked from Daniel's shoulder. "Abaft the beam!"

"He really does sound like a pirate," Daniel said.

"Double double," DaVinci said.

"Uh," Kimani said. "Is he saying what I think he's saying?"

"Doubloon!" DaVinci said, nipping at Daniel's hair. "Pretty!"

"Hey, Joy! Did you hear that?" Daniel looked for Joy in the hammocks, but she wasn't there. She was on her knees in front of the firepit. "What's she doing now?"

"Writing in the sand with a stick," Kimani said, slipping between two palm trees.

"Either that or making a sandwoman," Daniel said.

"Ta-da!" Joy said, tossing her stick away.

Daniel walked closer and read the message in the sand. "Sharktooth Island?"

Joy nodded. "Because naming our tropical paradise 'New Joyland' would be selfish."

"Sharktooth Island is cool," Daniel said.

"What about Dolphin Island?" Kimani said. "I love dolphins."

"Too late. It's official now!" Joy said. "It's written in the sand."

"Um, I'm not sure—" Kimani started.

But Joy kept talking, pointing past the firepit. "Check that out!"

Three green coconuts sat on a log bench beside a wreath of flowers.

"Finally!" Daniel said, as DaVinci launched from his

shoulder and swooped around the palm trees.

"I thought coconuts were brown," Joy said. "Why are these ones green?"

"They're young coconuts," Kimani said. "That means they have water inside."

"Even better than lemonade!" Joy said.

Daniel grabbed a coconut. "How do we open them?"

"I don't know," Kimani said, sitting on the log.

Daniel shook his coconut next to his ear and heard sloshing inside. "Cool."

"Cooler if we could open them," Joy said, thumping her coconut against the log. *Thump, thump.*

"Hey, DaVinci!" Daniel called. "Lend me your beak!"

"Boom boo-DOOM boom!" DaVinci squawked, flying in a bright yellow-and-blue streak between the trees.

Daniel gave his coconut a few whacks with his palm. *Doop, thoop. Doop.*

"Boom-thoom," DaVinci called.

From the jungle, other birds answered *eep-diddee-ee-twee,* and on the beach, the waves *crrasssh-swooshed,* and a rhythm started: *thump, doop, boo-boom, eep-diddee, twee-crrasssh.*

Then drums sounded all around them, fast and fierce and happy:

Boom-badoom-doom-boom-ba-BOOM.

Boom!

Boom-ba-doom-doom. Boom-ba-doom.

BOOM!

"Well," Joy said. "Here we go again."

Chapter 13

"You think this is our ride home?" Daniel asked.

The drumbeat sounded like it was coming from the jungle.

Badoom-BOOM-ba-boom! BOOM-ba-ba-doom!

Daniel peered into the foliage... and a shadow moved behind a flowering bush.

"I think I see someone!" he said.

"Where?" Joy asked, looking into the trees. Her eyes widened. "Oh, me too!"

Ba-da-BOOM-BOOM-ba-da-ba-badoom.

"Maybe it's the drummer," Daniel said.

"See you next time!" Kimani cried behind them. "Nice meeting…"

"What are you talking about?" Daniel asked, but when he turned, Kimani was gone.

The drums pounded louder and louder, faster and faster. The sunlight glinting on the waves seemed to flash brighter and brighter.

All at once, Daniel felt the ground drop away, like he was rocketing into the sky, and the drumbeat swallowed the world.

The blue sky vanished. The palm trees and coconuts disappeared. The beach and the islands were gone.

Then Daniel fell, gentle as a snowflake, into the wintry world of home. Snow swirled around him, and the warm beach became a freezing basketball court.

And Joy was there too, standing near her snowwoman, tucked inside her puffy winter coat and hat.

"You're in your jacket again," she told him.

"And I'm already cold." Daniel shook his head. "Where's Kimani?"

"Back in her library, I guess. Writing things down in her notebook."

"No way," he said. "There's no way that just happened."

"Way!" Joy said, just like DaVinci, as she zipped up her coat.

"Wait," Daniel said. "Stop!"

"What? Why?"

"You're still wearing the necklace!"

Joy touched the leather cord around her neck. "Whoa."

"I wonder if..." Daniel reached inside his jacket and felt the blue bead. "Yep, I've got mine too."

"My lucky headband's gone though," Joy said, touching her forehead.

"Yeah." Daniel smiled. "Did you really see the mysterious drummer?"

"I definitely saw someone," she said. "Behind that flower bush."

"I wonder what he wants," Daniel said.

"What did Kimani mean by 'see you next time'?" Joy asked.

"I don't know," Daniel said.

"Bet we'll find out soon," Joy told him.

Daniel raised his face to the sky. "I hope so."

Ordinary snow still fell across the city, ordinary cars still drove past the playground. School still started tomorrow, with the same old classrooms and the same old desks.

But the day felt different to Daniel and Joy. The *world* felt different. Something special swirled down among the snowflakes. Something magical.

ARE YOU UP TO THE CHALLENGE?

Ahoy, mateys! It's time for your very own Sharktooth Island challenge! Arrrrr ye ready to build a bridge that's strong enough to keep ye safe above shark-infested waters? That's right, build a bridge using gumdrops and toothpicks, ye will! Then you'll hang the bridge above a blue slime ocean filled with hungry paper sharks. Don't worry, you won't be walkin' the plank alone. Daniel, Joy, and Kimani are here to help you take on this challenge. Now, full STEAM ahead!

DANIEL'S THREE-POINT POINTERS

Hey, Challenge Island friends! I'm here to give you the game plan for building a bridge that is strong, steady, and up for the challenge!

My friends and I weren't in the mood to be fish food, so we had to figure out how to build a bridge that was strong enough to support each of us. We used bamboo twigs and clay to test out small-scale models before we built the real thing.

The secret to successful bridge building is knowing the right shape to use in your design. As it turns out, the triangle is a lot like my cousin Joy—small but mighty! It may not be the biggest, roomiest polygon in the math book, but the triangle is a geometric slam dunk!

Sure, the square seemed like a good choice for building our bamboo bridge, but when I tried to walk across it, the poles started creaking and cracking. We added a bamboo diagonally across the middle of each square and—ta-da!—the bridge got much stronger.

Try It!

First, make a square and a triangle using toothpicks and gumdrops. You will need 4 toothpicks and 4 gumdrops for the square, and 3 toothpicks and 3 gumdrops for the triangle. Put them together like this.

Test time! Let's start with the square. Try wiggling the sides and pushing in on the corners. Do you feel how wobbly it is? No wonder the bridge made of squares caved in under the force of my weight.

Now try the same thing with the triangle. Can you feel the difference? The sides don't budge. The corners don't wiggle. The triangle wins the strength test!

During this challenge, you can turn any square into two mighty triangles by connecting a toothpick diagonally across the middle, just like Joy, Kimani, and I did.

Kimani knew that a bridge made of triangles is called a truss bridge. A simple truss bridge, like this one, was just right to get me across the water to safety.

But what if you needed your bridge to be super-duper strong? I mean eight-lanes-of-cars-and-two-train-tracks strong! That's what the civil engineers who designed Sydney Harbor Bridge in Australia had to figure out. They had to create a bridge that could support 200,000 cars, trucks, and trains every day.

There is only one shape strong enough for that task! You guessed it—the unbreakable triangle.

Those engineers knew that to make the strongest structure possible, they had to use as many triangles as they possibly could. So that's what they did.

This is Sydney Harbor Bridge. Can you count how many triangles it has?

And here's what it looks like close up. How many triangles do you see now? Too many to count!

How Many Triangles?

Counting the number of triangles in Sydney Harbor Bridge would be a ginormous challenge. Notice how the bigger triangles are made up of smaller triangles, and many of the smaller triangles are made up of even smaller triangles. You could be counting those triangles forever! For fun, try figuring out how many triangles are in this diagram.

The answer is 13! Here's how I got it:

When you are building the bridge for your challenge, remember: the more triangles you use, the stronger your bridge will be. And *truss* me, you want your bridge to be as strong as possible to keep you above those hungry sharks!

The Joy of Bridge Building

Enough dilly-dallying with Daniel, Challenge Island friends. The waters are rising and (Yikes! Did you hear that splash?!) so are those hungry sharks! It's time to get moving on building that bridge of yours. The first thing to do is gather your supplies.

Make a Bridge

Supplies

- 1 bag of gumdrops
- 1 box of toothpicks (the round kind)
- 2 dining room chairs of the same height
- 1 small paper cup
- 1 paper clip
- Handful of "doubloons" (pennies will work too!)
- 1 pencil
- A few pieces of paper
- 1 ruler (or a piece of paper)

Set the STEAM Scene!

Take two chairs and arrange them so they face each other. If people were sitting in the chairs, they would be knee to knee. Move the chairs apart so there is about a foot (or 12 inches) of space between them. Measure with your ruler to get the right spacing. If you don't have a ruler, put a piece of paper on the floor longways, so the top is touching one chair and the bottom is touching the other. That's the right distance.

Sketch Your Design!

SPLASH! Yes, I heard that too, but there's no sense in building your bridge before drawing a picture of what it will look like. That would be like a pirate sailing the high seas without a map! When you draw your bridge idea, don't forget to use plenty of triangles in your design. And don't forget to also draw sharks in the water below!

Build Your Bridge!

Great work! Now it's time to build your bridge! Use the sketch of your design to guide you as you go, but don't worry if things don't look exactly like you thought they would. They never do!

Remember how we turned squares into triangles by putting a bamboo pole diagonally across the middle of the square? You can do the same with a toothpick. Keep adding length to your bridge until it's long enough to reach from the edge of one chair to the edge of the other.

Test the Strength!

Once your bridge reaches from chair to chair, check how strong it is. Make a strength tester by unbending a paper clip into an S. Poke one end through your paper cup and hang the other end from the middle of your bridge.

Once the cup is hanging from your bridge, put doubloons (or pennies) in, one by one. How many can your bridge hold before it starts to bend? Write down the number of doubloons on a piece of paper

Make It Stronger!

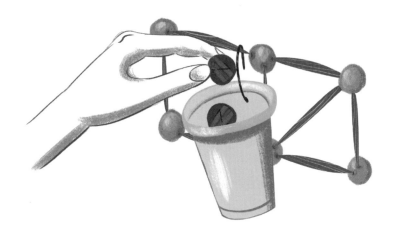

So, how'd you do? Were you able to fill up the whole cup with doubloons? Or did your bridge start caving in first? Either way, you can still make your bridge stronger. The most exciting part about engineering is that no matter how perfect the design may seem, there is always room for improvement and imagination!

Remember how the engineers of the Sydney Harbor Bridge used more and more triangles to strengthen their design? You can do the same! Try adding sides and a top to your bridge. Are there still some squares in your bridge that you could turn into triangles?

Test your bridge again. Does it hold more doubloons this time? If you run out of coins or space in your cup, set things on top of your bridge to test its strength. Can your bridge support an apple? What about a full soda can? Are you still safe from the sharks below?

Keep testing and improving your bridge.

Kimani's Shark Remarks

Daniel and Joy think all sharks are hungry for humans. The truth is, even if those fins had been sharks instead of dolphins, chances are we would have been just fine. In fact, we humans have a bigger chance of being injured by a toilet than by a shark!

There are actually more than 450 different kinds of sharks in the world's oceans. They come in all shapes and sizes, from the tiny 8-inch-long dogfish shark to the massive 40-foot-long whale shark. Most of these sharks are completely harmless to humans. It's true, your odds of getting chomped and turned into shark food are nearly 1 in 4 million.

Even a great white shark, the one with the worst rap of all, isn't all that dangerous to people. Great whites don't want to munch humans. They would rather snack on a juicy tuna or sea lion. Every now and then, they see a person jumping or swimming around in the water and confuse the person for a flapping seal. But like I said, you're more likely to get clobbered by a toilet seat.

Right before I got whisked off to Sharktooth Island, I was at the library reading a book about great whites and making this list in my notebook.

Kimani's Top 10 Fantastic Facts About Great White Sharks

1. Great white sharks have 300 teeth arranged in 7 rows. The teeth are razor-sharp, 2 inches tall, and shaped like (what else?) TRIANGLES!

2. Great white shark teeth fall out all the time and are replaced with shiny new ones. One shark can go through 30,000 teeth in its lifetime! No wonder we found so many washed up on the Sharktooth Island!

3. Baby great whites are called pups. They are about 5-feet long when they are born and have up to 12 brothers and sisters. The pups hatch from eggs while they are still inside their mama, then eat the unhatched eggs until they are born.

4. As soon as those great white pups are born, they swim away from their mother. If they don't, mama shark may try to eat them.

5. A full-grown great white is 15 to 20 feet long (as long as a giraffe) and weighs up to 5,000 pounds (as much as 14 gorillas).

6. Great white sharks have gray bodies and white bellies. These colors help camouflage them as they sneak up on unsuspecting prey or sea animals the shark wants to eat. Prey swimming above look down and see the sharks' gray tops, which are the same color as the darker water below. When prey from below look up, the shark's white bellies help them blend in with the sunlit water above.

7. Great whites have such a strong sense of smell that they can sniff out a sea lion 2 miles away and detect a tiny drop of blood from up to 3 miles away.

8. A hungry great white can launch itself out of the water and fly up to 10 feet in the air. This behavior, called breaching, allows them to catch fast-moving meals like speedy seals.

9. Great white sharks are shaped like torpedoes and can swim crazy fast through the water—up to 40 miles per hour! That's nearly highway speeds.

10. Great whites are the ultimate ocean predator and at the top of the food chain. The only sea animals strong enough to attack them are orca whales and other great white sharks.

DaVinci's Art Attack

Ahoy, lads and lassies! Wondering where I got me cool name? I'm named for one of the most famous artists EVER. Leonardo da Vinci painted his swashbuckling masterpiece, the *Mona Lisa*, more than 500 years back. But 10 million landlubbers a year still pile into the Louvre Museum in Paris, France, to see it. Shiver me timbers!

Da Vinci was a true artistic genius, but what many buccaneers don't know is that he was also a brilliant scientist and inventor. He sketched designs for airplanes, helicopters, and parachutes hundreds of years before they were invented! He mixed science, technology, engineering, art, and math together in a magical way. Ye might say that da Vinci was the original STEAM sea dog!

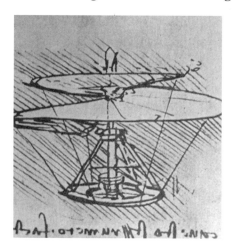

And speaking of STEAM, me hearties, it's time to add some Arrrrrrt to your STEM. Let's finish setting the scene for yer bridge with a sparkling blue ocean filled with circling sharks.

Make a Slime Ocean

Supplies

- ¾ cup clear glue
- 2 drops blue food coloring
- ⅔ tablespoon baking soda
- 1 tablespoon contact lens solution
  (must include boric acid and sodium borate)
- 1 mixing bowl
- 1 mixing spoon
- Glitter (optional)

Directions

1. Pour the ¾ cup of clear glue into a bowl.

2. Add 2 drops of blue food coloring. Mix with
   a spoon.

3. Add ⅔ of a tablespoon of baking soda to the
   bowl and mix well.

4. If ye are adding glitter, stir it in now.

5. Now add 1 tablespoon of contact lens solution and stir for 1 minute.

6. Leave the mixture alone for 2 minutes, then start kneading with your hands.

7. If the mixture is too sticky and doesn't come off your hands as you knead, add more contact lens solution or baking soda.

Make Some Sharks

Supplies

- Crayons or markers
- Scissors
- Glue or tape
- Clothespins
- Shark template (download and print at www.challenge-island.com/books)

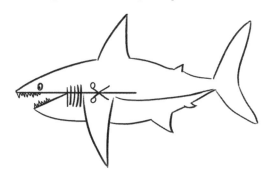

Directions

1. Color in the shark and use scissors to cut it out.

2. Glue or tape the back of the shark to the clothespin.

3. Cut the shark along the scissor line on the shark template so the mouth opens and closes.

4. Squeeze the clothespin to bring your shark to life.

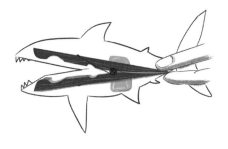

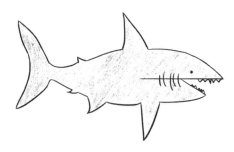

Put It Together

Finish setting the scene by spreading yer ocean goo out on a sheet pan and placing it on the floor below yer bridge. Position your sharks on and around the ocean slime.

Write down the number of doubloons your bridge can hold, put it next to your bridge, and take a picture of your whole scene!

Send your photo to: Books@challenge-island.com and we'll post it on our website at www.challenge-island.com!

Well done, mateys! You've completed the Sharktooth Island Challenge! But our STEAM voyages together are just beginning. We have many islands yet to explore and many more challenges yet to conquer.

Until next time...

Boom-ba-DOOM-boom-boom badoom!